Missing
Kitten

The Missing Kitten

by Holly Webb

Illustrated by Sophy Williams

For Emily and the gorgeous Rosie Bumble

tiger tales

5 River Road, Suite 128, Wilton, CT 06897
Published in the United States 2016
Originally published in Great Britain 2013
by Little Tiger Press
Text copyright © 2013 Holly Webb
Illustrations copyright © 2013 Sophy Williams
ISBN-13: 978-1-58925-488-6
ISBN-10: 1-58925-488-0
Printed in China
STP/1800/0090/0216

For more insight and activities, visit us at www.tigertalesbooks.com

Chapter One

Suzanne looked around her new bedroom with delight. It was huge! And as it was up in the roof of the cottage, it was a really interesting shape, all ups and downs. There was a beautiful window as well, with a curly handle to open it, and a big, wide windowsill she could sit on. Her old bedroom had been tiny, and a very boring, square shape.

"Good, isn't it?" Jackson, her big brother, poked his head around the door. He had the bedroom next to hers, which was basically the other half of the roof space. Mom and Dad had said that their bedrooms used to be the attic.

"I love it," Suzanne said happily. "The window's the best thing! I love seeing all the fields and trees, and look! Cows! Out my bedroom window!"

Jackson chuckled. "Cows, not cars. Now *that's* a change! Yeah, it's really good. Except everything's pretty far away."

Suzanne nodded slowly. "There is a store in the town," she reminded him.

Jackson made a face. "Yeah, one store! And a blacksmith. How weird is that?"

"And the school's in the town, too," Suzanne added, very quietly. "I wish we didn't have to change schools." That was the thing she was least happy about with their move to the countryside. She was really going to miss her old school, and her friends. Lucy and Ella had said they'd come and stay over the next vacation, but that was a long time away. And meanwhile, she was going to start at a school where she didn't know anyone, and she certainly didn't have any friends.

"It'll be all right," Jackson told her cheerfully, and Suzanne sighed. He wasn't worried. He never was. Jackson was really sporty, and he found it very easy to make friends. And yet he didn't show off, so people just wanted to hang out with him. Suzanne wished she knew how he did it.

"Did you hear that rustling noise?" Jackson pointed up at the ceiling. "I bet there are mice in all that thatch. Remember to tell Mom and Dad about that, Suzanne. You need to start working on them again about a kitten, now that we're here. They said maybe after we'd moved, didn't they?"

Suzanne grinned at him. "I know! I thought I'd maybe give them a day, though, before I started asking. Let them get some boxes unpacked first...." She looked up, too. "Do you really think there are mice?"

Jackson gazed thoughtfully at the ceiling. "Probably. It sounds like it to me. Unless it's a rat, of course."

"Ugh! Okay, I'll ask Mom now. No way am I living in a house with a rat!" Suzanne shuddered.

"I'm with you on that," Jackson grinned. "Rats can be pretty big, you know. Bigger than a kitten, anyway." He made a rat-like face, pulling his lips back to show his teeth.

"Stop it!" Suzanne cried. "Maybe we can get a grown-up cat then. I don't mind if it isn't a kitten. I'd just love to have any kind of cat and they did say maybe we could. You'll help, won't you? You'll ask, too?"

Jackson nodded. "Yeah. Although I don't like the idea of coming down in the morning to find a row of dead mice on the doormat. That's what Sam says his cat does."

Suzanne looked worried. "I think I'd rather have a cat that just scares the mice away...."

Suzanne started her kitten campaign while everyone was sitting down eating lunch. It felt really odd seeing their old table in a completely different kitchen.

"It's so quiet," Mom said happily, looking out the open window. "I don't think I've heard a single car since we got here. I love that we're down at the end of the road."

"I keep thinking there's something missing," Dad admitted. "But it'll be great once we're used to it. And the air smells amazing."

Jackson sniffed loudly. "That's the cows, Dad."

Suzanne made a face at him. She didn't want him distracting Mom and Dad—this was a great opportunity to mention a kitten. She took a deep breath. "It's not a bit like Edward Street, is it?" she said, thinking about their old home. "With all the traffic...." She swallowed, and glanced hopefully from Mom to Dad and back again. "You wouldn't worry about a cat getting run over here, would you?"

Dad snorted with laughter and turned to Mom. "You win, Laura. She lasted more than an hour."

Suzanne blinked. "What do you mean?"

Mom reached out an arm and hugged her around the shoulder. "Dad and I were talking about it last night, Suzanne. We wondered how long you'd be able to wait before you asked about a cat. I said that I thought it would be once we'd settled in a bit, and Dad said you'd ask the moment we got here. So I won, and now he has to cook dinner tonight!"

"Simple. Take-out pizza," Dad said, taking a huge bite of sandwich.

Mom smiled at him. "You do realize it's a 20-minute drive to the nearest store, now, don't you?"

"You mean you were just waiting for me to ask? So, can we have one?" Suzanne said hopefully, eager to get back to talking about kittens.

Mom nodded slowly. "Yes. But we can't go off to an animal shelter tomorrow—we need to do some unpacking, and besides, I don't have a clue where the closest one is."

"I could find out!" Suzanne said eagerly. "It's just—it would be really nice to have time to get to know the kitten before school starts. We only have two weeks, and then Jackson and I won't be home for most of the day."

Dad nodded. "I know, Suzanne, but

I don't think we'll be able to find you a kitten right now. I know it would be wonderful to have one while you're still at home. But it won't be a huge problem if you're at school. Mom'll be at work, but I'll be at home, so the kitten won't be lonely. And your new school's really close. You'll be home in 10 minutes."

Suzanne nodded. That was another thing that was different, being able to walk to school. Mom and Dad had even said she and Jackson could walk by themselves, if they wanted, since there were sidewalks the entire way.

"I suppose." Suzanne nodded. "So, we can really have a cat? You actually mean it? We can look for one?"

"Promise," Dad told her solemnly.

Suzanne beamed at him. She could come home from school and play with her cat. Her own cat! She'd wanted to have one for so long, and now it was going to happen.

"Suzanne! I'm off to town," Dad yelled up the stairs.

Suzanne shoved an armful of T-shirts into the drawer and dashed out of her room. "I'm coming!"

She really wanted to walk there. They'd seen the town a couple of times before. The first time was when they came to look at the house. Mom had gotten her new job at the hospital, and Mom and Dad explained that they would need to move, since it was too far for Mom to drive every day. Suzanne had really missed her for those few weeks when she'd been leaving early and not getting back until it was almost time for Suzanne to go to bed. Now that they'd moved, the hospital was only half an hour away, in Longwood, the nearest big town to their tiny little town, which was called Longwood Hills. Once they'd made the decision that Mom would take the job, and agreed to buy the cottage, Suzanne and Jackson had gone for a day's visit at their new school and seen the small town again. But Suzanne had been so nervous about the school that she couldn't remember what it was like.

"It's so pretty," she said, as they

walked along the sidewalk. "Look at all the flowers. I saw a rabbit last night, Dad, did I tell you?"

"Only about six times! I almost had a heart attack when you screamed like that. I thought you'd fallen out the window."

"Sorry! I was excited! I've never seen a rabbit in my yard before!" Suzanne giggled. "Can we go down here? Is it the right way?"

Dad nodded. "Yup, this is the quickest path down to the town, the way you and Jackson will go to school, probably."

Suzanne swallowed nervously. She was still worrying about the school. It was tiny, which was nice, she supposed. There wouldn't be that many people to get to know. But they'd probably all been together since preschool. They might not want a stranger joining their class at all.

Dad nudged her gently with his elbow. "You had a good time on your visit, didn't you?"

Suzanne looked up at him, surprised.

"It was pretty obvious what you were thinking, sweetheart."

"I suppose. Yes. Everyone was nice. But that was just one morning. I have to go there every day...."

"It'll be great. You'll be fine, I'm sure you will."

Suzanne nodded. She didn't really want to think about it. "Look—is that the town? I can see houses." She ran on ahead. "And there's the store, Dad, look."

"I'd better find the list," Dad muttered, searching his pockets. "We definitely need bread. Can you be in charge of finding that for me? Now where on earth did I put that list?"

But Suzanne wasn't listening. She had seen something—a bulletin board in the store window. It was full of advertisements—exercise classes in the church hall, someone offering to make celebration cakes, an almost-new lawnmower for sale....

And a litter of kittens, three black-and-white, one tabby, ready to leave their mother now, free to good homes.

Chapter Two

"Dad! Look!" Suzanne was so excited, she couldn't stand still—she was dancing from foot to foot, pointing madly at the flier.

"What?" Her dad hurried up, peering into the window. "Oh! I can see why you're so excited. 'Ready now,' hmmm?" He read the flier thoughtfully, and then took out his phone.

"Are you going to call them?" Suzanne squeaked excitedly.

"No. I'm going to put the number into my phone, get some bread and milk, and go home and talk it over with your mother. Can you imagine what she'd say if we went out for groceries and came home with a kitten?"

Suzanne sighed. "I guess you're right. It would be funny though." She giggled. "'Hi, Mom, here's the milk....' And we take a kitten out of the bag!"

"It might have been here a while, this flier," Dad pointed out. "The kittens might already be gone. Don't get your hopes up, okay?"

Suzanne nodded. But as they paid for the groceries, she took a deep breath and smiled at the lady behind the counter. She hated talking to people she didn't know, but this was important. "Excuse me, but do you see the flier in the window about the kittens? Has it been up for long—I mean, do you know if there are any left?"

The lady beamed at her. "You'd like a kitten, hmm? Julie Mallins will be happy. She only put the flier up earlier this week, and I know she's still looking for homes for all of them."

"Really?" Suzanne was dancing around again. She just couldn't help it. "Oh, Dad, can we go home and talk to Mom about it now, please?"

"All right, all right!" Dad grinned, raising his eyebrows at the lady.

Suzanne ran all the way home—in fact, she went twice as far as Dad did, because he wouldn't run, so she kept having to turn around and run all the way back to him to tell him to hurry up. When she raced in through the front door of the cottage, she was completely out of breath.

"Mom! Mom!" she gasped, running from the living room to the kitchen and back to the bottom of the stairs.

"What's the matter, sweetheart?" Her mom backed out of the cupboard under the stairs, where she'd been putting coats and boots away.

"Mom, there's someone in town who has a litter of kittens that they want to give away!"

"Really?"

"There was a flier up in the town store." Dad came in, holding out his phone. "I have the number. What do you think?"

Suzanne bit her lip to keep herself from shrieking "Please, please, please." Her mom was very firm about not whining, and she really didn't want to get on her mom's bad side right now.

"Well, I suppose we could ask to go and look at them...," her mom said, rather doubtfully. "I'm just a little worried because the house is all upside down right now while we're still unpacking. Wouldn't that be stressful for a kitten?"

Suzanne's face fell. Mom was right. "Maybe we could wait?" Suzanne whispered. "Maybe we could just choose a kitten and ask them to keep it for us a little longer?" She really wanted to have a kitten now, but she didn't want their new pet to start out scared by all the boxes everywhere.

Dad hugged her. "Well, let's see what Julie says—she's the owner," he explained to Mom. "She might not think it's a problem. To be honest, we've done most of the unpacking in the kitchen already. We could keep the kitten in there for the time being—I think you have to keep new kittens in one room to start off with, anyway."

Mom nodded. "I'd forgotten that. We used to have a cat when I was little," she told Suzanne, "but that was such a long time ago. We'll all have to learn how to take care of a cat together."

"What?" Jackson put his head around the kitchen door. "Are we getting one? What's happening?"

"Suzanne found a flier about a litter of kittens needing homes," Dad told him. "We should have known—if there were kittens around, Suzanne was bound to find them! Should I call this lady, then?"

Mom nodded, and Suzanne flung her arms around her. She held her breath and listened as Dad made the phone call.

"Hi, is this Julie? We saw your flier about the kittens.... Mmm.... We wondered if we'd be able to come and see them. Uh-huh. Well, now's great, if that's really okay with you. Fantastic. Spruce Street. Oh, off the main road? See you in about 10 minutes, then."

Suzanne gasped. Ten minutes! Ten minutes until they saw their kitten!

"Here they are."

Julie turned out to be a really sweet lady who'd adopted Goldie, the kittens' mom, after finding her eating scraps of bread under her bird feeder because she was a stray, and so terribly hungry.

"It took weeks to even get her to

come inside," Julie told Suzanne, as she led them through to the kitchen. "But she's settling down now. I think she knew she needed to let someone take care of her, so she could have her kittens somewhere nice and warm."

"How old are the kittens?" Suzanne's mom asked as Julie opened the kitchen door.

"Ten weeks—the vet said they should be fine to go to new homes," Suzanne heard Julie say. But she wasn't really concentrating. Instead, she was staring at the basket in the corner, where a beautiful brownish tabby cat was curled up, with four kittens piled around and on top of her.

"Goodness, she looks tired," Mom said.

"Yes, I think she is, poor thing. She's been a really good mom, but she was so thin to start with, aside from her huge tummy full of kittens. I was worried that she wouldn't be able to feed them, but she's done very well. They're all practically weaned now—they love their food!"

Woken by the voices, one of the kittens popped his head up, his big orange ears twitching with interest.

"Oh, look at him!" Suzanne whispered. "His ears are too big for him!"

Julie nodded. "I know, he's cute, isn't he? He has big paws, too; I think he's going to be a really big cat."

The kitten gently nudged the brother or sister next to him with the side of his chin, and the rest of the kittens popped up in a line, staring at Suzanne and Jackson.

The other three were black-and-white, very pretty, without the massive ears. They had enormous whiskers instead—great big white mustaches.

"I like the orange one," Jackson said. "That one's a boy, right?"

Julie nodded. "Yes, and the three black-and-white ones are girls."

"I like him, too," Suzanne agreed. "Will they let us pet them? Is that okay?"

"They're usually very friendly. Especially Ginger."

"Oh, is that his name?" Suzanne tried

not to sound disappointed. She would have liked to choose a name together for their kitten—Ginger was what all orange cats were called!

"Oh, no. I've tried not to give them names—I'm hoping to find homes for them all, and if I name them I'll just want to keep them. But it's hard not to think of him as Ginger."

The orange kitten was standing up now, arching his back and stretching as he climbed out of the basket. He looked sideways at Suzanne with his big blue eyes to check that she was admiring how handsome he was as he stretched. She was watching him eagerly, and she gave a little sigh of delight as he stepped toward her, gently rubbing himself against her arm.

"Oh, he has boots!" Suzanne looked over at Jackson and her mom and dad. "Look, he has furry white boots on!"

Mom laughed. "He does look like he has boots on," she agreed. "Those are very cute."

"I know lots of cats have white paws, but I've never seen one where the white goes that far up before." Suzanne petted the tabby kitten lovingly, and his black-and-white sisters followed him out of the basket, looking for some attention, too. Their mother stared watchfully after them, and then seemed to decide that Suzanne and the others weren't dangerous to her babies. She gave a massive yawn, and curled up for a nap.

The girl kittens let Suzanne's mom and dad pet them, then they took off chasing after a feathery cat toy, racing around the kitchen and batting it ahead of them with their paws. The orange kitten watched them, but he didn't join in. Instead, he placed a hopeful paw on Suzanne's knee, and she looked back at him, just as hopefully. Did he want to be picked up?

"He's very cuddly," Julie said quietly. "He's a real people cat. Try and put him on your lap."

Suzanne gently wrapped her hands around his fluffy middle. Even though he was the biggest of the kittens, he still felt tiny—so light, as though there was nothing to him.

The kitten gave a pleased little squeak, and padded his fat white paws up and down her jeans as though he were testing how comfy she was. Suzanne found herself smoothing her jeans, wanting him to think she was nice to sit on. He padded all the way around in a circle a couple of times, and then wobbled and flopped down, stretching his front paws out, and flexing his claws gently in and out of the denim fabric of her jeans.

"That tickles!" Suzanne giggled, petting him under his little white chin.

The kitten purred delightedly. That was the best place, the spot he was always itchy. He pointed his chin to the ceiling and purred louder, telling her to keep going.

Jackson joined in, running one finger gently down the kitten's back. "His fur's really soft. And look at his paws! They're bright pink underneath!" The kitten was enjoying the petting so much that he'd collapsed into a happy heap on his side, purring like a motorboat.

Suzanne looked down at his paws and laughed—they really were pink. A sort of pinkish-apricot color, and so soft and smooth-looking.

"They'll probably get darker once he starts going outside," Julie explained. "They've only been indoors so far. He'd need to stay in for a little longer if you decide to take him." She looked at Suzanne's mom and dad.

Suzanne and Jackson got up, then both turned to look at them, too, and their mom laughed. She turned to Julie and asked hopefully, "I don't suppose you could give us some cat litter, could you? The store in town would have cat food...."

"You mean we can take him now?" Suzanne gasped.

Her mom shrugged and smiled. "Why not?"

Chapter Three

"Dad, we're almost out of Boots's food. There's only the salmon flavor left, and I don't think he liked that one very much."

Boots wrapped himself lovingly around Suzanne's legs. He knew very well what was in those cans, and he didn't see any reason why he shouldn't have a second breakfast.

Calling him Boots had been Jackson's idea. Suzanne had suggested Sam, but it was like Ginger—a little bit too ordinary for such a special cat. Boots was much better.

Jackson looked up from his huge pile of toast. "We could go to the store," he said. "I've almost finished the bread, and there's not a lot for lunch."

"I've got a work call in a few minutes," said Dad. He looked at them thoughtfully. "Though I suppose you two could go, if you'd like."

"On our own?" Suzanne stared at him.

"Why not? You were going to try it when school started next week, weren't you? Just be careful, and stick together."

Suzanne shut her eyes for a second at

the mention of school. She was trying not to think about it. "Will you take care of Boots while we're out?" she said seriously.

"Suzanne! You'll only be gone half an hour!" Dad grinned.

"But he's not used to me not being here!" It was true. Suzanne had spent all of her time with Boots since they'd brought him home, only leaving him at night, when he was safely tucked in his cardboard box, on an old towel, and next to a hot water bottle to feel like his mother and the other kittens. Just until he got used to them not being next to him.

"I think it would be good for him to see you go out," her dad said gently. "I know you don't want to think about school, Suzanne, but you do go on Monday. Boots has had a whole week of you around all the time. He needs to learn to be without you."

"But he'll be lonely," Suzanne said worriedly.

"It's only for half an hour," Dad reminded her.

"When we're back at school it won't be!"

"Then he'll have me for company while I'm working. And you know how he loves the computer."

Suzanne smiled. It was true. Boots was fascinated by Dad's computer. He seemed to love the way the keys went up and down. He would sit watching Dad type forever, just occasionally putting out a paw to try and join in. Then he would look annoyed when Dad told him no. Secretly Suzanne was planning to let him try one day when she was using the laptop that she shared with Jackson. She wanted to see what Boots would write—she knew it would probably be a string of random letters, but she was hoping for a secret message!

"Come on, then." Jackson stuffed the last of the toast into his mouth. "Can we get some chips when we're at the store, Dad?"

"Sure. Here." Dad gave Jackson some money. "But I do want change. Be back by ten thirty, all right? I don't want to be pacing up and down outside looking for you."

"Are you really worried about school?" Jackson asked Suzanne as they wandered down the sidewalk in the direction of the town.

"A little." Suzanne sighed. "What if nobody talks to me?"

"Why wouldn't they?" Jackson asked, shrugging.

Suzanne shook her head. He was trying to be nice, but he just didn't get it.

"You had lots of friends at your old school," said Jackson. "Why do you think you won't make friends here?"

"It's such a little school," Suzanne tried to explain. "Only one class in each grade, and not that many kids in each class, either. They'll all know each other so well. Like I know Lucy and Ella." She wished she were as confident as Jackson.

He'd already managed to go out for a walk and found a couple of boys playing football. He'd joined in, and then he'd gone back to their house. Suzanne wasn't sure how he did it.

Jackson rolled his eyes. "Come on. We're almost there."

They went into the store, and Jackson went to look at football magazines, while Suzanne found the cat food. Then she realized that there were a couple of other girls standing behind her.

"Who's she?" one of them whispered.

"Don't you remember? It's that new girl. The one who came to school for a morning."

"Ohhh! What's her name?"

"Something weird. Amber or something."

Suzanne felt like her stomach was squeezing into a tiny knot inside her. She was the one they were talking about. The girl with the weird name. She wanted to scream, "Suzanne!" But she didn't. She grabbed a couple of cans of cat food, and scooted over to where Jackson was.

School was going to be a disaster. It was so obvious.

Suzanne lay in bed, watching her clock creep closer to seven. She'd been awake for a while, worrying about their first day at school, and now she just wished it would hurry up and be time.

A throaty purr distracted her, and a soft paw patted her chin. Boots liked her to be paying attention to him, not the clock.

"I'm glad I went downstairs and got you before breakfast," Suzanne said, tickling him behind the ears. "I know I look miserable, but you're making me feel a lot better."

Boots closed his eyes happily and purred even louder. Suzanne knew all the places he liked to be petted, and how he particularly liked being on her bed. It was much cozier than his basket.

"I'm really going to miss you today," Suzanne murmured. "I hope you'll be okay. Dad will take care of you." She sighed, a huge sigh that lifted up the comforter around her middle, and Boots's ears twitched excitedly. He wriggled forward, and peered down under the comforter. It was like a dark little nest, and he wriggled into it, just his tail sticking out, and flicking from side to side.

"What are you doing?" Suzanne giggled. "Silly cat! Oh, Boots, you're tickling my legs!"

Even the tail had disappeared now. Boots was a plump little mound traveling around under the comforter. Then he popped out at the other end of the bed, his orange fur looking all spiky and ruffled up. He shook himself and ran a paw over his ears.

Suzanne twitched her toes under the comforter, and he stopped washing and pounced on them excitedly, jumping from side to side as she wriggled them.

"You're awake!" Mom poked her head around the door. "Time to get up, Suzanne. Hello, Boots." She came in and patted him. "Are you worried that he'll miss you while you're at school?"

Suzanne nodded, and Mom hugged her. "It'll be fine, sweetheart. Now that he's allowed in the yard, he'll probably just go out and try to chase butterflies again." She looked at Suzanne. "And you'll be fine, too. Honestly. Try not to worry about it."

Suzanne nodded. But she wished she felt as sure as everybody else seemed to.

Boots sat on the back doorstep, next to his cat flap, staring around the yard. He was confused, and a little bored. Suzanne had gone somewhere. He'd known that she was going—she had picked him up and made a huge fuss over him before she went, and her voice had been different than normal, as though something were wrong. But he hadn't expected her to be gone this long.

He stalked crossly around the yard, sniffing at the grass, looking for something interesting to do. He sharpened his claws on the trunk of the apple tree, and tried to climb it, but he wasn't all that good at climbing yet, and he only got halfway up before he got worried and jumped down again. Then he had to sit and wash himself for a while, pretending that he'd never meant to climb it in the first place.

Where was she? Jackson was gone, too—he preferred to play with Suzanne, but Jackson was very good at inventing games with sticks, and pieces of string to chase.

Why had they gone away and left him? And when were they coming back?

Chapter Four

"Boots! Did you miss me?" Suzanne picked him up, and hugged him lovingly, and Boots rubbed his head against her cheek.

Dad had come to meet them from school, as it was the first day, but tomorrow they were going to walk there and back by themselves.

"Come and have a cookie," Dad

suggested. "Then you can both tell me what it was like, now that there's no one else around." When he'd asked Suzanne at the school gate how her day was, she'd just muttered, "Fine," but he could tell she was only being polite.

"It was all right." Jackson shrugged, munching a chocolate cookie. "Played football at lunch. The teacher was a little strict. Shouted at people for talking. But it was fine."

Dad looked over at Suzanne, who sighed. "It was okay. This girl named Izzie was told to show me around, and she was nice. She took me with her at recess and lunchtime. But—well, it was only because she had to."

"She might really like you!" Dad pointed out.

Suzanne ran one of Boots's huge ears between her fingers, and sighed. "Maybe…. It wasn't as bad as it could have been," she admitted. The two girls she'd seen in the store hadn't said anything else about her weird name, which was what she'd been worrying about. They'd been at the same table as Izzie and her at lunch, and they'd been friendly, and asked her where she lived, and if she took the bus to school.

It turned out that lots of the students did—they came from several different towns, and a school bus went around and picked them all up.

"It's nice that we can walk to school," she said to Dad, who was still looking worried about her.

Boots rubbed himself against her red sweater, leaving orange hairs all over it, and Suzanne petted him again. Whatever happened at school, at least she could come home and play with him. She couldn't imagine being without him now.

"You're sure you wouldn't like me to come with you?" Dad asked for about the fourth time.

"No!" Jackson said. "Honestly, Dad. We're fine. It takes about 10 minutes to get to school, and we don't even have to cross a road. Stop worrying."

Boots was sitting on the bottom step of the stairs, watching disapprovingly as Suzanne and Jackson got ready. They were going again, just like yesterday! Why was he being left behind? He let out a tiny, furious meow, but Suzanne only kissed the top of his head, and went out the door, leaving him with Dad.

Dad picked Boots up, and tickled his ears, before rubbing the top of his head. But then he put him back down on the stairs, and headed into the room where his computer was. He was going to be too busy to play, again.

Boots stalked into the kitchen and inspected his food bowl, which was empty. He had a little water, and looked at his basket. He didn't really feel like sleeping. And if this were anything like yesterday, Suzanne and Jackson would be gone for hours.

He didn't see why he couldn't go with them. Until yesterday, he'd been with Suzanne almost all the time.

Boots walked over to the cat flap and sniffed at it, carefully. They hadn't been gone long. Maybe, if he was quick, he could follow them. Boots shot out of the cat flap and dashed into the back yard. Suzanne and Jackson had gone out the front door, so he hurried around the side of the house, and on to the front yard. He nosed his way under the blue gate, flattening himself underneath the wooden panels, and coming out into the road, next to the car. His whiskers twitched excitedly as he tried to figure out which way Suzanne had gone. He could follow her scent, he was sure. He sniffed busily at the grass, and then set off running.

Suzanne and Jackson were halfway to school, walking down the sidewalk along the side of the big field, when suddenly, she stopped.

"Can you hear a meow?" Suzanne asked, and Jackson turned around to stare at her.

"Don't be silly. Come on!"

"No, I can hear meowing. I really can. It's Boots, I'm sure." Suzanne peered along the sidewalk behind them and laughed. "It is! Look!"

Boots was running after them, meowing happily, and as Suzanne crouched down to say hello, he clambered up into her lap and sat there, purring wearily. He'd had to run faster than ever before to catch up.

"What's he doing here?" Jackson shook his head. "Yes, you're very clever, Boots," he admitted, running one hand down the little kitten's back. "But now we have to take you  back home, and we're going to be late."

"Do we have to take him back?" Suzanne asked sadly.

Jackson rolled his eyes. "Yes, of course we do! We can't take a cat to school, Suzanne!"

"I suppose not."

"And we have to run, because we're going to be late."

Suzanne swallowed anxiously. She didn't want to be late, to have to go in after everyone else, and explain what had happened. They hurried back down the sidewalk and across the street before bursting through the front door.

Dad came out of his office, looking worried. "What's the matter? Why are you back? I knew I should have gone with you!"

"Don't worry, Dad. Everything's fine." Suzanne held out her arms, full of purring tabby kitten. "Boots just followed us. He caught up with us as we were going past the big field. We had to bring him back." She put Boots into Dad's arms, and he stopped purring and glared at her. He'd gone to find her, and brought her back, and now she was going again!

"Sorry, Boots. I'd much rather stay with you." Suzanne petted his head as she turned to leave.

"Come on, Suzanne!" Jackson yelled from the door.

"You'd better run, sweetheart," Dad said. "I'd drive you, but driving would take longer than walking the short cut. I'll call the school and explain why you'll be a little late, don't worry."

"Thanks, Dad," said Suzanne.

When Suzanne and Jackson hurried onto the playground, the principal, Miss Wilson, was standing at the main door watching for them.

Suzanne was worried. Luckily, Miss Wilson didn't look angry. She just smiled at them as they raced toward her, and patted Jackson's shoulder. "Don't worry. I used to have a dog that followed me to school. Still, I've never heard of a cat doing it. He must be very fond of you."

Suzanne nodded proudly. She hadn't really thought of it like that.

"I explained to your teachers what happened, so just slip quietly into your classes, all right?"

"Thanks, Miss Wilson." Suzanne crept, mouse-like, along the hallway. It was all very well to say to slip in quietly, but everyone was still going to turn and stare at her. She eased open the door of her classroom, wincing as it creaked.

But her teacher, Mrs. Mason, just smiled at her and waved her over to her table, and went on pointing out something on the whiteboard.

"I wondered where you were!" Izzie whispered to her. "I thought you might not be coming back!"

"It wasn't that bad yesterday," Suzanne muttered.

"Are you okay?" said Izzie. "Did you

oversleep?"

Suzanne shook her head. "No. It sounds really silly, but I had to take my kitten home. He followed us to school."

"Your kitten did?" Izzie stared at her. "I didn't know you had a kitten! I've got a cat. His name is Oscar. But he's never followed me anywhere! He's too lazy. What's your kitten's name?"

"Boots." Suzanne smiled proudly. "We've only had him two weeks, and he isn't used to us leaving him. Mrs. Mason's giving us a look. I'll tell you more at recess, okay?"

Izzie grinned. "You're so lucky to have a kitten."

Suzanne nodded and stared at the whiteboard. Izzie was right, she realized. She really was lucky.

Chapter Five

"I'll keep Boots inside until after you've left," Dad said at breakfast the following morning. "If I don't open the cat flap for an hour or so, and I give him a lot of attention, I'm sure he'll stay put."

"I hope so," said Mom anxiously. "We don't want him to wander too far. If he starts going out in the road and along the sidewalks, he could easily get lost."

She glanced up at the clock. "I'd better get going. Have a wonderful day, all of you. Suzanne, do you want to invite that nice girl from your class to come over after school one day? What was her name? Izzie? I can call her mom. Maybe she could come tomorrow."

Dad nodded. "I can pick you all up from school."

Suzanne smiled. Dad had been so happy when she'd come home the day before and said she'd actually had a good day at school. She would really like Izzie to come over.

"I'll ask her," she agreed, tickling Boots behind the ears. He was sitting on her lap, hoping for bits of toast. He particularly liked toast with jelly, so Suzanne made sure she always had

jelly on at least
one piece now.
She tore off a
little corner,
and passed it
down to him,
watching him crunch it
up and lick at his whiskers for crumbs.

"Do you really think Boots will be
all right?" she asked Dad anxiously.
"I don't want him to be lonely."

A cautious paw reached up onto
the table, looking for more toast, and
Dad snorted. "He'll be fine. He knows
how to take care of himself very well.
Don't you?" he added, scratching Boots
under his little white chin. "Yes, you're
so cute. Even if you are trying to steal
yourself a second breakfast."

Boots drooped his whiskers, and stared at Dad, his blue eyes round and solemn.

Suzanne giggled. Boots made it look as though he were starving to death and even Dad was almost convinced. He glanced down at his own plate of toast, and then shook his head firmly.

"That kitten is a clever one!" he told Suzanne.

Boots prowled up and down the hallway, his tail twitching angrily. Suzanne had left him behind again, and now his cat flap was closed. He didn't understand what was happening. Why did she have to keep going away?

"Hey! Boots! Cat treats!" Suzanne's dad came out of the kitchen with a foil packet, and Boots turned around hopefully. He loved those treats, especially the fish-flavored ones. "Good boy. Yes, Suzanne said some of these might cheer you up."

Boots laid his ears back as he heard Suzanne's name, and stopped licking the treats out of Dad's hand. Suzanne! Was she about to come back? He looked at Dad hopefully.

"Oh, Boots. You really do miss her, don't you?" Dad eyed him worriedly. "She'll be back later, I promise. Come on, yummy fish treats."

Boots ate the rest of the treats slowly. He liked them, but he would have liked them much more if Suzanne had fed them to him. She had a game where she held them in front of his nose, one at a time, and he stretched up to reach. They didn't taste the same out of Dad's hand.

"Good boy, Boots." Dad picked him up gently, took him into the office, and put him down on an old armchair. "Why don't you take a nap?"

Boots walked around and around the seat of the chair, pushing his paws into the cushions, until eventually he slumped down and stared gloomily at the door. He didn't feel like sleeping, but he couldn't think of anything else to do.

Boots sat in front
of the cat flap,
staring at it hopefully,
and uttering plaintive
little meows. It was still
locked. He knew because he'd
tried it, over and over, scratching
at the door with his claws. But it just
wouldn't open.

"Do you need to go out?" Dad asked,
coming into the kitchen, and looking
at him, concerned. He crouched down
next to Boots, who gave his knee a
hopeful nudge. "I suppose it can't hurt.
It's been more than an hour since
Jackson and Suzanne left for school."
Dad turned the latch on the cat flap
and pushed it, showing Boots that it
was open. "Go ahead."

Boots meowed gratefully, and wriggled through the cat flap, trotting purposefully out into the back yard, and straight around to the front of the house, just as he'd done the day before. Next, he was squeezing under the gate, and out into the road. This time he didn't run as fast. He knew that he'd been shut in the house for a long time, and he wouldn't be able to chase Suzanne the way he had yesterday.

So he padded down the path, sniffing thoughtfully here and there. It was difficult to follow the traces of Suzanne and Jackson—the house smelled like them, too, much more than the path, which made it confusing. But he was pretty sure that they'd gone this way. Boots bounded happily along, hoping that they would be in the field again, maybe sitting down, waiting for him.

But no one was there. Boots walked up and down the edge of the huge field, staring anxiously into the green stalks. Was Suzanne in there? She might be, but he couldn't smell her, or hear her. He slipped in between two rows of wheat, pushing his way through the green stalks, and meowing.

Then his ears twitched. There was a scuffling noise ahead of him, and a small bird fluttered out of the wheat, making Boots leap back in surprise. He'd seen birds in the yard, but never up close. He hissed at it angrily, but the bird was already half-hopping, half-flying away. Boots followed it sadly out of the wheat stalks. He didn't think Suzanne was here.

Glancing around the narrow path at the edge of the field, he tried to remember what Suzanne had been doing when he ran after her yesterday. They had been walking along here, away from him, as though they were heading for the hedge at the end of the field.

Determinedly, Boots padded along, hopping over the ruts and big clumps of grass, and keeping a hopeful eye out for Suzanne. At the corner of the field there was a gap in the hedge, and then a short muddy path, leading out on to a road with a sidewalk. Boots had never really seen a road, and he jumped back, his whiskers bristling, as a car roared past. He had been in a car when he left his mom to come to Suzanne's house, and then when he'd had to go to the vet for his vaccinations, but both times he had been in a cat carrier. From kitten height, the cars going along the road were enormous, and terrifyingly noisy.

He crept into the muddy path, eyeing the opening out on to the sidewalk. His ears were laid nervously back, but at the same time Boots breathed out the faintest little purr. The cars weren't the only noise he could hear. There was shouting, and laughter—the kind of noises Suzanne and Jackson made. He wasn't sure it was them, but it was worth looking. The sounds were coming from very close by. If he was brave enough to go out on to the sidewalk, close to those cars, he was sure he could find the place.

Boots dashed out, scurrying along low to the ground, and pressing as far into the hedge as he could go. Every time a car went past—which wasn't very often, thankfully—he buried himself under the prickly branches at the bottom of the hedge and peered out, his blue eyes round and fearful.

The school was only a couple of hundred feet along the main road through the town, and on the same side as the path. Boots squirmed under the metal fence at the side of the playground, and scuttled behind a wooden bench, where he sat, curled up as small as he could, and watched the children racing around the basketball court.

It was very noisy. He had thought Suzanne and Jackson were loud, but there were so many children here. And they were all wearing the same red cardigans and gray skirts, or shorts. He couldn't see Suzanne at all.

He shrank back behind the bench as a loud bell shrilled, and the children streamed back into the building on the far side of the playground. Then his ears pricked up, and he darted forward. That was Suzanne! Racing past him, with another girl. He meowed hopefully at her, but she'd already disappeared inside the white building.

The door was still open.

Boots padded out into the empty playground and hurried over to the door. The noise of the children still echoed around the hallway, and he shivered a little. But if he wanted to find Suzanne, this was where he needed to be. He padded along the chilly concrete floor, peeking in the doors when he found an open one. The first classroom he looked into was full of children who were smaller than Suzanne, he thought. A little boy stared at him, and pointed, his eyes widening delightedly. Boots scooted out the door as fast as he could. He had a feeling that he wasn't meant to be in here, and he didn't want to be caught before he'd found Suzanne.

The next couple of doors were shut, but then he found one ajar and looked around it. These children were more the right size. He sidled around the door, and then he saw her, facing away from him, but at the nearest table. The children were all looking away from the door, toward something at the other end of the classroom, so it was easy for Boots to race across the carpet and hide under the table—right next to Suzanne's feet. He purred quietly to himself. He had done it! He'd found her!

Very gently, he rubbed the side of his head against Suzanne's sock.

Suzanne gave a tiny squeak, and Izzie stared at her. "What's the matter?"

"Something under the table...," Suzanne whispered, her eyes horrified. It was furry. What if it was one of those enormous furry spiders? There were definitely more spiders in the country. She'd found a huge one in the bathroom over the weekend. Very slowly, she peered under the table, and Izzie looked, too.

"A cat!"

"Boots!"

Mrs. Mason looked around sharply, and Izzie and Suzanne tried to look at the board and pretend there wasn't anything under their table.

Boots purred louder, and patted at

Suzanne's leg with a velvety paw.

"What's he doing here?" Izzie whispered as soon as Mrs. Mason had turned back to the board.

"He must have followed us again." Suzanne was grinning. She couldn't help it. She wasn't quite sure how she was going to figure this out, but she loved it that Boots wanted to be with her so much that he followed her all the way to school.

Boots scrambled up on to her lap and sat there, purring, and nudging at her school cardigan.

Sarah and Missy saw a small orange head sticking up over the edge of the table and gasped. Suzanne put a finger to her lips and stared at them, pleading. "Don't tell!" she whispered.

Sarah and Missy shook their heads, to say of course they wouldn't. But Mrs. Mason had seen them anyway.

"Suzanne, what's going on?" She came over to their table. "Oh, my! A kitten! What's he doing here?"

"He followed me from home," said Suzanne. "I'm sorry, Mrs. Mason. He was under the table, and I didn't even know he was here until a minute ago."

She sighed, a very tiny sigh. She'd hoped to keep Boots a secret for a little longer.

Mrs. Mason smiled. "Well, he's very sweet, but I'm afraid he can't stay in the classroom. You'd better take him to the office and ask Mrs. Hart to call home. Is there someone who can come and get him?"

Suzanne nodded. "My dad." She stood up, with Boots snuggled against her, and the rest of the class whispered and aahed admiringly, reaching out to pet him as she went out of the classroom.

"You're so amazing for finding me!" Suzanne whispered, and Boots purred.

Chapter Six

"I can't believe you followed me all the way, Boots!" Suzanne told him again, as she cuddled him in between putting her shoes on for school the next day. "Everybody wanted to know about you. Even people in the grade above came to ask who you were—they saw me carrying you up to the office on their way back from PE." She sighed, and placed him down on the stairs so she could put on her other shoe. "But Miss Wilson made Dad promise he wouldn't let it happen again. He said Miss Wilson was really scary. You're going to hate being shut up for the whole day." She petted his head, looking at him worriedly. "I suppose in a few days you'll stop wanting to follow me. But I sort of wish you wouldn't. I love that you're so clever!"

Boots clambered up a couple of steps—it took a little while, as his legs were still pretty short—so that he could rub his chin on Suzanne's hair while she tied her shoe. He wasn't sure what she was saying, but it was definitely nice. She was fussing over him, and he liked to be fussed over.

Jackson came stomping down the hallway, and Suzanne turned around and dropped a kiss on the top of Boots's little furry head. "I've got to go. Be good, Boots!"

Boots sat on the steps and stared at her angrily as she slipped quickly out the front door, pulling it closed behind her. She had done it again! How many times did he have to follow them before she decided it would just be easier to take him with them? He jumped down the stairs in two huge leaps and ran for the cat flap. But it was locked. He scratched at it furiously until Dad came and picked him up.

"Sorry, Boots. Not happening, little one."

Boots wriggled out of his arms and stalked across the kitchen. He was going to follow Suzanne— somehow.

He would have to get out of the house a different way. Boots prowled thoughtfully through the different rooms, sniffing hopefully at the front door to see if it might open. He could smell outside, but the door was firmly shut. And so were all the windows.

But when Suzanne had taken him upstairs to play the day before, her window had been open. Boots sat at the bottom of the stairs and gazed upward doubtfully. They were very big. But he could do it, if he was careful, and slow.

Determined, he began to scramble and haul himself up, stopping every once in a while to rest, until at last he heaved himself onto the landing. His legs felt wobbly, but he made himself keep going into Suzanne's room, where the door was open just a crack. As soon as he pushed his way around the door, his ears pricked forward excitedly. The window was open! Just as he had remembered it!

Forgetting how tired his legs were, Boots sprang up onto the bed, sniffing delightedly at the fresh air blowing in.

The windowsill was too far above the bed for him to reach, though. His whiskers drooped a little. How was he going to get up there? He padded up and down the bed and stared at Suzanne's pile of cuddly toys. She liked to tease him with them, walking them up and down the bed for him to pounce on. But why shouldn't he climb up them instead? He put out a cautious paw, testing the back of a fluffy toy cat. It squashed down a little, but it was still a step up, and then onto the back of a huge teddy bear, and the stuffed leopard … and the windowsill!

Boots pulled himself up, panting happily as he felt the cool breeze on his whiskers.

Now he just had to get down again on the outside....

"No kitten today?" Sarah asked Suzanne a little sadly.

Suzanne shook her head. "Miss Wilson made my dad promise he'd keep him in. Poor Boots. He's going to be so upset."

"He's the cleverest cat I've ever seen," Sarah told her admiringly. "Imagine coming all that way! And he'd never even been to the school before—I don't know how he figured out where to go!"

Suzanne smiled. "It's amazing, isn't it? I think he must have heard us all in the playground."

"You should stop by the store and buy him a treat on the way home," Izzie suggested. "I've got some money, if you don't have any on you."

Suzanne nodded. "It's okay, thanks. I've got some. That's a really good idea." She grinned at Izzie. "You can help me choose." It was so nice having a good friend to hang out with—it felt like being back at her old school. Izzie's mom had been fine with Izzie walking with Suzanne—Izzie usually walked home, too. She had an older sister in Jackson's class.

"He might even start talking to us if we bring him cat treats…."

Boots scrambled frantically at the branches of the bush. It had looked so solid and easy to climb. But it turned out to be much harder to get down than up. It was also more wobbly, and he didn't like that. The first part had been easy, just a little jump to that sloping part of the roof, then across the tiles. It was the drop down from the roof that was the problem. His claws were slipping. Boots gave up trying to hang on and leaped out, as far away from the wall as he could, hoping that he remembered how to land.

He hit the ground with a jolt, but he was there! In the front yard, right by the gate and the road. Boots darted a glance behind him. Then he scrambled under the gate and set off to find Suzanne, trotting along jauntily. He knew the way now; he didn't have to sniff and search and worry.

He was halfway down the field when it started to rain. A very large drop hit him on the nose, making him shrink back. It was soon followed by a lot of others, and in seconds his fur was plastered flat over his thin ribs. He hid in the hedge, his ears laid back.

He would wait for it to stop, Boots decided, gazing out disgustedly. He certainly didn't want to go anywhere in that. But it went on and on, and he needed to find Suzanne. He put his nose out cautiously, and shivered as he felt the drops on his whiskers. It was horrible.

But he couldn't stay here all day….

At last he slunk out from under the bush, plodding through the wet, muddy ruts, and hoping that Suzanne would have something warm and dry to wrap around him when he got to the school. He scurried down the pavement, through the puddles, so miserable that he didn't even bother to dart under the bush to avoid the car going past. The driver of the car didn't see the soaked little kitten, and even if he had, he probably wouldn't have been able to avoid the huge puddle that splashed up over Boots like a wave. There was so much water that he staggered back, letting out a cold, sad meow. Then he flat out ran for the school, racing across the playground toward that warm, open door.

But it was closed.

It had been wet at recess, and no one had wanted the rain blowing in. All the doors were closed—every single one, as the soaked, orange-striped kitten found when he ran frantically all the way around the building.

Remembering the window he had climbed out of at home, Boots looked up to see if there were any he could get through. There was a bench up against the wall, with a window right above it, and he jumped for the seat, scrambling desperately until he could heave himself up. Then it was a little hop onto the arm of the bench,

and then again onto the windowsill.
But the window was shut, and
everyone was gathered together at
the other end of the classroom,
looking at something and talking
excitedly. They didn't hear him
scratching hopefully at the window,
and at last he jumped down.

Boots sat under the bench and meowed miserably, calling for someone to come and let him in. He didn't care if they took him back home again, as long as he was out of the rain. He would stay at home, and never try to follow anyone, if only he were dry.

No one came. No one heard him over the hammering and splashing of the rain, and the water from the bench was dripping all over him. Boots crawled out, looking around for another place to hide. There were trees over on the edge of the path to the field. Maybe it would be drier there. He ran through the wet grass, shivering as the stems rubbed along his soaked fur, and shaking water drops off his whiskers. He was so cold. Sitting still under the bench had made him shiver, and now he couldn't stop.

Then something made his ears flick up a little. There was another building. Just a little one, a shed, and he could see that the door was open!

Boots made one last effort, forcing his shaky paws to race to the shed, and struggle over the step and into the dusty dryness. He was so relieved to be out of the rain that he hardly noticed the sports equipment piled up all over the place— just the heap of old, tattered mats that he could curl up on to take a nap.

It was while Boots was fast asleep that the custodian remembered that he hadn't locked up the shed when he'd taken out the extra chairs, and came grumpily back through the rain with his keys.

Chapter Seven

"Boots!" Suzanne called happily, as she opened the front door to let herself and Izzie and Jackson inside. "Boots, come and meet Izzie!"

Dad hurried out of the kitchen, a worried expression on his face. "You didn't see him in the road?"

Suzanne stared at him, not understanding. "What?" she asked, with a frown.

"Boots! He's not out there? I wondered if he'd slipped out somehow. He must have, because I can't find him anywhere." Dad glanced distractedly up and down the hallway, as though he thought Boots might pop out from behind the boots.

"You—you can't find him?" Suzanne stammered. "You mean—he's lost?"

"I'm sorry, Suzanne." Dad ran his fingers through his hair until it stood up on end. "I had a long phone meeting all morning that finished about an hour ago. Then I went to find Boots and check that he was all right, but he'd disappeared. I just don't understand how he could have gotten out!"

"Maybe he didn't," Izzie suggested

shyly. "He could be shut in somewhere. Oscar's always doing that. He climbed into a drawer once and went to sleep, and my mom didn't see him and she shut the drawer. Then she got a real shock because her dresser was meowing."

"Maybe…," Dad murmured. But he looked doubtful. "Let's check again."

Suzanne grabbed Izzie's hand and pulled her up the stairs, while Jackson hurried into the living room.

"Bathroom," Suzanne muttered. "Not in here. The linen closet, maybe?" She pulled the door open, but no kitten darted out. "Jackson's room…." She peered in and called, "Boots! Boots! He isn't here, Izzie. I'm sure he'd come if he heard me calling. Or he'd meow to tell me where he was."

"He could be asleep. Try the other rooms, just in case."

Suzanne peered into her mom and dad's room, opening the dresser and all the drawers, but there weren't even any orange hairs. "This is my room," she told Izzie, pushing the last door open. "Boots!" Suzanne caught her breath. She'd been hoping to find him asleep on her bed, but he wasn't there.

"Your window's open…," Izzie said slowly.

"Oh, but he couldn't get out through that." Suzanne shook her head. "It's really high."

Izzie frowned. "It depends how much he wanted to."

The girls climbed onto the bed so that they could look out the window.

"You see? He could jump on there."
Izzie pointed toward the low part of
the roof. "And there's all that ivy stuff.
That's like a cat ladder."

Suzanne stared at her. "You think he
really could have climbed down that?"

Izzie looked down at the grass, which
was a very long way down. "He might
have."

Dad came in, with Jackson behind.
"He isn't in the house," Dad said grimly.
"Was that window open, Suzanne?"

"Yes!" Suzanne nodded, her eyes filling
with tears. "I'm really sorry, Dad!
I didn't think Boots would try
to climb out of it! He can hardly
get up the stairs, and
the windowsill's
really high."

"It isn't your fault." Dad put an arm around her. "I should have checked on him earlier. None of us realized he would be able to climb out of the window." He leaned over to look out. "I think he did, though. Some of that bush has been torn away."

"Can we go and look for him?" Suzanne asked. "He might have tried to get to school again, and gotten lost…. Oh, Dad, what if he went out on the road?"

Dad hugged her tighter. "Don't panic, Suzanne. I don't think he would, because he's scared of the car noises. Remember how he meowed when we got him out of the car at the vet? Even though he was safe in his basket, he didn't like it when the cars went past. And why would he get confused about the way to school, when he made it yesterday?" He let go of Suzanne and headed for the door. "I'm just going to call the school and see if he's turned up there."

Suzanne sank down on her bed, staring up at Izzie. "I can't believe it. Everyone's been telling me today how lucky I am, and how beautiful Boots is, and now he's gone. I've only had him a couple of weeks, Izzie! How could I have lost him?"

It was starting to get dark. Boots scratched at the door with his claws again, but they were starting to hurt. He'd hoped that he could make that little thin strip of light and fresh air bigger, maybe even big enough to squeeze through. But all he'd managed to do was scratch off some of the paint. Miserably, he sank down, meowing faintly. No one seemed to hear him, and it had been a long time since he'd last heard anyone outside.

Maybe he would have to stay here all night, he thought anxiously. Suzanne wouldn't know where he was. Maybe she was looking for him. He stood up again quickly, even though his paws felt sore, and meowed as loudly as he could. Suzanne would look for him, he was sure of it.

But even though he called and called and called to her, she didn't come, and at last he had to give up. He was worn out from scratching and meowing, and he dragged his sore paws back to the pile of mats. Then he curled up into a tight little ball and lay there in the gathering darkness, wondering how long it would be before anyone found him.

"We can make some 'lost' posters," Izzie suggested the next morning. "If we ask Mrs. Mason, I bet she'll let us use the computer to make the fliers. We could put them up all around town on the way home."

Suzanne nodded. She should have thought of that the night before. After Izzie had gone home, she and Jackson had searched the house all over again, and then Suzanne had gone to bed and cried herself to sleep, knowing that her little kitten wasn't curled up in his basket in the kitchen—he was out there in the dark, and she had no idea where.

"We could go to the houses between here and school and ask if anyone's seen him," she suggested, shivering at the thought of poor Boots wandering around lost somewhere.

"Good idea," Izzie agreed. "We could get people to check their garages. Don't worry, Suzanne. I can help with that. I know almost everybody in town, and it's scary if you don't know people."

"That would be great," Suzanne said. She'd do anything if it meant finding Boots, even if she had to talk to hundreds of people she didn't know.

A couple of the middle-school girls came past Suzanne and Izzie on their way in. "Hey, Suzanne! Did you get into trouble with Miss Wilson yesterday?" one of them asked.

Suzanne stared at her in bewilderment. "W-what?" she muttered, suddenly shy.

"When your kitten came back! I thought your brother said that Miss Wilson was angry, and she told your dad that he had to keep your kitten at home."

Suzanne forgot all about being shy. "You mean you saw Boots? Are you sure it was yesterday?" she asked the older girl eagerly.

"Yeah, definitely...." The older girl—Suzanne was pretty sure her name was Emma—frowned. "I saw him looking in the classroom window, but then he ran off. Why? What's the matter?"

"Boots is lost," Suzanne explained. "Dad had him in the house, but he climbed out of a window. We think he must have tried to follow us. We weren't sure he had made it to school, but if you saw him, then he was definitely here!"

"You're not mixing up the days?" Izzie asked Emma doubtfully.

Emma shook her head. "Nope. I'm certain. It was yesterday when it was raining. And your kitten was soaked. His fur was actually dripping. I saw him out the window; he was in the playground. Before recess, I think."

"He must have gotten out the window really soon after we left," Suzanne said. "Thank you, Emma! I have to go and look for him!"

Chapter Eight

There was sunlight coming in from somewhere else, Boots noticed, as the shed grew slowly lighter that morning. It wasn't just the space around the door. Where there was light, maybe there was some sort of hole, or another window that might be open, so he could climb through it.

It was up at the top, near the ceiling,

he saw. Very high up. Much higher than Suzanne's window. But then, there were a lot more things to climb in here. Piles of chairs, some benches, and more of those mats. He'd just have to find a way to reach it.

Boots was sure that Suzanne was looking for him—almost sure, anyway. But the shed was all the way across the field from the school, he'd realized, as he lay curled up on the mats. What if Suzanne didn't know about it? He couldn't wait for someone to let him out. He would have to do it himself.

He stretched out his paws, which felt a little better this morning, though they still ached from all that scratching. Then he padded across the pile of mats, and made a wobbly jump onto an old wooden bench. That was the first step....

"Where do we start?" Izzie asked, as they hurried across the playground.

"I don't know. Maybe we should find Jackson and tell him that those girls saw Boots," Suzanne suggested, but she couldn't see her brother anywhere, and she wanted to start searching. "My dad called yesterday, remember? And he spoke to Mrs. Hart in the office, and she asked in the staff room. No one had seen Boots. So he wasn't just hanging around school looking for us."

Izzie frowned. "I know I keep going

on about him being shut in somewhere, but…."

Suzanne shook her head. "No, I think you're right! It's the only thing that makes sense. But where?"

Izzie shook her head. "I don't know. Maybe the classroom closets? Do you think if we asked Mrs. Hart we could go and look? Oh, no! There's the bell."

Suzanne looked anxiously around as everyone began to collect his or her stuff and head into school. "I can't go into school now! I can't! Boots is here somewhere. I know he is!"

Izzie patted her shoulder. "It's okay. Look, we'll tell Mrs. Mason that Boots might be here. We have to go in, Suzanne. Otherwise, we'll get in trouble."

Suzanne almost didn't care, but she supposed Izzie was right. Maybe they could ask the principal what to do. She'd said her dog used to follow her to school. She'd understand.

But Miss Wilson was talking to one of the other teachers, and she just waved the girls past when Suzanne tried to hover in the doorway and talk to her.

Mrs. Mason was late coming into their class, and when she finally arrived she had her arms full of colored shirts for PE, and she didn't look like she wanted to hear about kittens, even though Izzie tried her best.

"Oh, dear.... Well, I'm sure you can take a look at recess," she said distractedly when the girls tried to explain. "Sit down, please, you two."

Sit down! Suzanne opened her mouth to argue, but Mrs. Mason wasn't even looking at her anymore.

"Once I've taken attendance, everyone, I've got some exciting news— we're going to start practicing for Sports Day. We've scheduled a couple of extra PE sessions, and the first one is this morning. So let's just mark everyone here...." She moved names around on the whiteboard. "Where's Keisha? Is she still sick? Okay."

"I don't want to do PE," Suzanne whispered frantically. "I have to go and look for Boots!"

"PE!" Izzie nudged her. "I just thought of something! Shut up in a shed, Suzanne—we said he might be!"

"What are you talking about?" Suzanne was fighting back tears.

"There's a little shed at the end of the field where Mr. Larkin, the custodian, keeps stuff that doesn't get used very often. He was definitely carrying chairs in and out yesterday; I heard him complaining about how wet he'd gotten."

"So the shed was open?" Suzanne breathed, her eyes widening.

Izzie nodded. "It must have been."

"Now go and get changed, please, everyone," Mrs. Mason called. "Then we'll go to the gym, as it's still a little too wet on the field."

"I'm not getting changed," Suzanne

said, glaring at Izzie as though she thought her friend might argue. "I'm going to find Boots."

Izzie shrugged. "Uh-huh, and I'm coming with you. Come on."

They hurried out of the classroom, ahead of everyone else, and Izzie grabbed Suzanne's hand. "It's this way. There's a side door; come on." She pulled Suzanne down the hallway and pushed open a door that Suzanne hadn't even known about. "This is a quick way out to the field."

"Hey, Izzie!" someone called. "We're in the gym, not the field! And you aren't changed!"

But Izzie and Suzanne were already running across the damp grass.

Boots wobbled on the old chair. He was almost there—he could see the narrow wooden windowsill and the dirty pane of glass. The wind was shaking it, as though it were loose. If he could only get to it, maybe he could push his way out, somehow....

He balanced himself again, teetering on the edge of the chair. He'd scrambled his way up the whole pile, and it had taken so long. If he misjudged his jump to the window, he wasn't sure he'd have the strength to climb up again. He was so hungry, and tired, and his paws hurt.

His whiskers flicked and shook as he tried to figure out how he could make the jump. It was much further than he'd ever jumped before. And the strip of wood along the window was very small. But if it meant that he could get out…. Then he would go back home, and wait there for Suzanne. He would see if he could get back in through the cat flap.

He tensed his muscles to spring, and crouched there, trembling a little, trying to summon the courage to leap.

Then his ears twitched. He could hear someone! People, talking!

"Boots! Boots, are you in there? Is the door locked, Izzie?"

That was Suzanne!

Boots let out a shrill, desperate meow, and forgot to worry about how narrow the ledge was. He just went for it, scrambling madly with his paws as he almost made it, and then heaving himself up onto the windowsill.

Then he batted his paws against the glass, meowing frantically.

"I can hear him! He's in there, Izzie! You were right!"

"It's locked. I'll go and get Mr. Larkin."

Boots heard feet thudding away and cried out in panic. They hadn't heard him! They were leaving!

"It's okay, Boots. Where are you?"

There were noises outside and Boots banged his nose against the grubby window, trying to see what was happening.

Suzanne pulled herself up onto the tiny ledge on the outside of the window. "I can see you! It's really you, Boots! Oh, I've been so worried. I can't believe you climbed out of a window." She giggled with relief, and sniffed. "And now you're trying to climb out of this one, aren't you, silly kitten."

Boots meowed and scraped, but the window wouldn't open. How was he going to get to Suzanne?

"Oh! Mr. Larkin! The keys!" Suzanne's face disappeared from the window, and Boots wriggled himself around as the door rattled and shook. And then it opened.

With a joyful yowl, he bounded back to the wobbly chair, and took a flying leap to the mats, and then Suzanne was there, hugging him.

Boots purred and purred, and rubbed his face against hers, and purred louder.

"Izzie! Suzanne! What are you doing out here? Oh! Oh, no, has he been shut in here?" Mrs. Mason peered worriedly into the dusty shed.

"All night," Suzanne told her, shivering. "Can I call my dad, Mrs. Mason, please? Can I take him home?"

Mrs. Mason nodded. "Yes, you'd better take him up to the office again. I hope he doesn't keep doing this, Suzanne."

Suzanne petted Boots, who was pressed against her sweater like he never meant to let go. "Me, too."

"Well, he got soaking wet and trapped in a shed, so maybe he'll stay home now," Izzie suggested.

Suzanne nodded. "He looks like he wants to go home," she agreed, feeling the sharp little points of Boots's claws hooked into her sweater. "I promise I won't ever let you get lost again," she whispered to him, feeling his whiskers brush across her cheek. "I'll take care of you forever."

"I'm really glad my mom said I could come back with you." Izzie sighed happily and blew on her hot chocolate.

Suzanne nodded, petting Boots, who was curled up on her lap, with his claws hooked determinedly into her school skirt. He wasn't letting her go. "We might never have figured out where he was if it hadn't been for you! He could have been stuck in there for a really long time—until Mr. Larkin had to put the chairs away again."

Boots purred as Suzanne gently rubbed behind his ears. He was finally starting to feel warm again. Suzanne's dad had lit the fire in the living room, and the girls were huddled in front of it—it was raining again, so it had been a wet walk home. They'd splashed through the puddles as fast as they could, anxious to see Boots again, and check that he was okay.

"Do you want any more hot chocolate, girls?" Dad asked. "Jackson's getting another cup."

Suzanne shook her head. "No, thanks."

Izzie smiled at him. "No, that's okay, thanks. It was delicious. It's too bad that cats can't have hot drinks, though. Boots must have been frozen after spending the night in the shed."

"I've had him on my lap ever since I picked him up," Dad told them. "Except for when he was wolfing down a huge dinner and breakfast in one. He definitely wanted company, and since he couldn't have you, Suzanne, I was the next best thing."

"I hope he's not going to follow us again tomorrow," Suzanne said, looking down at him anxiously. He didn't look very adventurous at the moment....

Dad shook his head. "No, I'm sure he'll remember being trapped. He won't want that to happen again. But I promise I will make sure every window's closed. I'll even let him play with the computer, Suzanne." He grinned. "I'll find him one of those homework websites. Then he won't need to go to school."

Boots stretched out his paws and stared up at everyone in surprise as they laughed, and then once again he curled himself into the front of Suzanne's sweater. It was cozy and warm inside. And dry. He hadn't realized how damp and miserable it could be, following people. For the moment, he was going to stay right here.